THE OWL-TREE

Joe ... es the magical owl-tree. But can he save it from
bei... cut down? Find out in this enchanting story.

JENNY NIMMO worked at the BBC for a number of
years ending in a spell as a director/adaptor for
Jackanory. Her many books for children include
The Night of the Unicorn, *The Stone Mouse* (highly
commended for the Carnegie Medal and broadcast on
BBC TV), *The Owl-tree* (winner of the Smarties Book
Prize), *Toby in the Dark*, *Dog Star* and *Tom and the
Pterosaur*. Her well-known trilogy, comprising *The Snow
Spider* (winner of the Smarties Book Prize), *Emlyn's
Moon* and *The Chestnut Soldier*, was made into a
television series. Jenny lives in a converted watermill in
Wales with her artist husband and occasionally her three
grown-up children. At present she is working on the
seventh book in the Children of the Red King series, the
popular stories about Charlie Bone and his friends.

THE OWL-TREE

Written by
JENNY NIMMO

Illustrated by
ANTHONY LEWIS

WALKER
BOOKS

First published 1997 by Walker Books Ltd
87 Vauxhall Walk, London SE11 5HJ

This edition published 2007

2 4 6 8 10 9 7 5 3 1

Text © 1997 Jenny Nimmo
Illustrations © 1997 Anthony Lewis
Cover illustration © 2007 Anthony Lewis

The right of Jenny Nimmo and Anthony Lewis
to be identified as author and illustrator respectively of this
work has been asserted by them in accordance with the
Copyright, Designs and Patents Act 1988

This book has been typeset in Plantin Light

Printed in Great Britain by Creative Print and Design (Wales), Ebbw Vale

British Library Cataloguing in Publication Data:
a catalogue record for this book is available from the British Library

ISBN 978-1-4063-0518-0

www.walkerbooks.co.uk

In memory of Marcus Crouch

CHAPTER ONE

When Granny Diamond took Joe into the small back-bedroom his heart sank. It seemed so dark and chilly. But then she drew aside the curtains and said, "Look, Joe! The owl-tree. Now that's a view worth having."

"The owl-tree?"

Through the window Joe saw a great sweep of leaves. Red, green and gold – they changed colour in the wind and fell in bright showers over Granny Diamond's garden. There were no trees like it near his home in the city and a little stab of wonder made him gasp. "It's so big," he said. "Why d'you call it the owl-tree?"

"A long time ago I saw an owl there," Granny

Granny drew aside the curtains and said, "Look, Joe!
The owl-tree. Now that's a view worth having."

Diamond told him. "It was perched on one of the high branches and framed by the moon. I was feeling a bit down at the time, and the owl lifted my spirits."

"Did you see it again?"

"Oh, yes, often. And then it vanished and I began to wonder if I'd really seen it, or whether it just flew into my head to cheer me up."

"I think the owl was real," Joe said.

"Maybe, but now my owl-tree keeps me going. I look at it every day. It's such good company."

Good company? She spoke as though the tree were a friend who talked to her. Was it enchanted? Joe stared hard at the tree and noticed that although the branches swept over Granny Diamond's lawn, the trunk began on the other side of her wall. "It isn't *your* owl-tree," he remarked. "It's growing in the garden next door."

"The branches are mine. They're on my side of the wall." His gran sounded a bit testy.

Joe saw a movement under the tree. A man in a dark hooded coat was raking up leaves. "Who's that?" He nodded at the man.

"My neighbour, Mr Rock," his gran said, rather coldly.

"The owl-tree belongs to him!"

"Don't say that, Joe." Granny Diamond backed away, mouth buttoned tight, eyebrows beetling. "Tell your sister tea'll be ready in half an hour."

Have I said something wrong? Joe wondered.

He ran across the passage to his sister's room. Minna was sitting on the bed under the picture of an angel. The angel was pale and golden-haired, but Minna was dark. She had a bothered, brooding look.

"Why are you cross?" Joe asked. "You got the room you wanted."

"I'm not cross," snapped Minna. "I just wanted to be at home when the baby comes."

Their mother was in hospital, expecting a new baby. It was already a week late. Everyone had been too busy to look after Joe and Minna for half term. Everyone except Granny Diamond.

"I'm glad we're here," Joe said. "There's an owl-tree outside my window."

He expected Minna to ask what an owl-tree was,

Minna was sitting on the bed.
She had a bothered, brooding look.

but she didn't even seem curious. "What's so great about an owl-tree?" she muttered, picking up a book.

Joe gave a loud sigh. He hoped his sister wasn't going to be moody all week. She was older than he was, older and braver. She fought for what she wanted and nearly always got it.

He went back to his room and looked down into the garden next door. Mr Rock was still there. He was staring at the owl-tree and, although his face was hidden, Joe could tell that he wasn't smiling. There was something grim and unfriendly about the tall, motionless figure.

All at once the tree shivered violently, tossing a cloud of tiny birds into the air. And Joe knew that the owl-tree was afraid of Mr Rock.

CHAPTER TWO

"Gran, are you friends with Mr Rock?" Joe asked at teatime.

"No," she replied. "My neighbour keeps to himself."

"Does he look like one?" asked Minna. "A rock, I mean."

"Well…" Granny Diamond hesitated. "He looks a bit strange," she said at last.

"Why?" For the first time that day Minna looked cheerful. "Does he have a funny nose, or horns?" She waggled two fingers above her head. "Or wicked red eyes? Is he old?"

"He's about the same age as I am," Granny Diamond said. "And, as a matter of fact, he's a very brave man. A hero. He was a fighter pilot in the war, and his plane was shot down in flames."

"Whee – oo – crash!" cried Minna, raising and dipping her hand like an aeroplane.

"Did that change him?" Joe asked gravely.

"It did." Granny Diamond frowned at Minna, whose two hands were now fighting each other over her head. "It's made him rather … unsociable. I've tried to be friends, but it's no use."

Joe couldn't finish his meal. He kept seeing a man tumbling out of the sky. Joe was afraid of falling. It was why he never climbed trees, like Minna did.

Granny Diamond understood. "You two go off and play," she said. "I'll see to the dishes."

It was too dark to go outside. Joe stood at the sitting-room window while Minna watched television. Eerie sounds crept through the dusk: a human sort of hooting, then laughter, then a scream and three glittering clusters of light bobbed away from the house next door.

"Minna, look!" said Joe.

Minna came to the window. She squinted at the

bobbing lights and suddenly exclaimed, "It's Hallowe'en! The journey and everything made me forget. Come on!" She raced out of the front door calling, "Wait for us!"

The three lights moved down the lane to Granny Diamond's gate and a voice croaked, "Trick or treat?"

"I'll fetch Gran. She'll give you a treat!" Minna twirled away but as Joe made to follow her, she commanded, "Joe, wait here!" So Joe waited, though he would rather have followed his sister. It was dark in the lane and the figures were shrouded in ghostly white sheets. The light came from flickering candles in the hollow pumpkins they held. The pumpkins had glowing carved-out skull faces.

Joe knew there were children beneath the white sheets, though he couldn't see their faces in the mysterious fluttering light. One of the figures said "Hello!" and pulled the sheet away from his head. "How d'you like living next door to a monster?" he asked.

"A monster?" Joe took a step backwards.

Another sheet came off another head. Now Joe

The light came from flickering candles in the
hollow pumpkins they held.

could make out two boys taller than himself, with pale curly hair.

"A monster," the second boy repeated in a harsh whisper.

"Why is he a monster?" Joe shuffled further away from them.

"He's got a scary face," said the first boy. "He growls and he's mean."

Joe didn't have time to ask more. Granny Diamond came out with a tray of orange juice and hot pies. Beside her, Minna held a lantern to light the way, and when she drew close the ghosts began to look more human. Joe could see two freckled faces with identical grins.

"Treats for ghosts," said Granny Diamond, laying her tray on top of the wide stone wall. "Ghosts, meet Joe and Minna."

"Hi!" The twins burst through the gate, grabbing for pies, and when the smallest ghost let his shroud fall back, Joe saw a serious boy with pale hair like the others, but without curls or a smile.

"These are the Ludds," Granny Diamond told Joe

and Minna. "Roger, Ian and Alex. Have you visited my neighbour?" she asked the boys.

While silent Alex shook his head one of the twins said, "We didn't … like … go in. We just did a bit of haunting."

"Tch! Tch! Now if you'd knocked properly, you might have got a treat."

"Never," said Roger. "Not from him."

Minna set the lantern on the wall and cartwheeled round the dark garden, surprising the twins, who watched in awed silence and then asked, "Will you be here for bonfire night? There's going to be a party on the green." They took no notice of Joe. Serious Alex darted anxious looks at the monster's house, while munching his pie.

"We might be here." Minna stood upright, hands on hips, getting her breath back.

"Everything comes at once," said Granny Diamond. "Ghosts, bonfires and new babies."

The Ludds swallowed their last crumb and ran off calling, "We've got five more hauntings to do. Thanks, Granny Diamond. See you, Minna!" They hadn't said another word to Joe.

Minna and Granny Diamond went back to the house, but Joe took a few steps closer to the wall that ran between the two front gardens. He peered up at the monster's house. There were no lights on at all. No flickering blue television, no firelight. Did Mr Rock sit alone in the dark, then? What did he do?

That night Joe lay awake in his strange room wondering if, one day, he would be like Minna. Would he ever be funny and brave and surprising? He wasn't at all sleepy. He felt like running down into the garden. But he made do with jumping out of bed to see if there was a moon.

The sky was bright with stars, the moon half hidden behind the tree. In the next-door garden a long rectangle of light sparkled on the frosty grass. A tall shadow moved into the patch of light and loomed towards the owl-tree.

The tree shivered and its frozen leaves made a strange, melancholy sound. Joe ran back to bed. Why was the tree so frightened of the monster?

CHAPTER THREE

Minna was full of ideas next morning. They poured out over breakfast. She wanted to make a Guy, collect wood for a bonfire, build hurdles to jump over, walk to the village, climb a hill and visit the Ludds.

Joe and Granny Diamond listened in silence as the list grew and Minna's plans became more ambitious. When she drew breath, at last, Granny Diamond managed to say, "You can't do all that today, Minna."

"What shall I start with, then?" she asked.

Joe suggested collecting twigs. He thought it was something he could take part in.

"OK," Minna agreed. "We'll start in the back garden."

They had hardly cleared breakfast before she was outside kicking up leaves, swooping on twigs and

Minna was full of ideas next morning.
They poured out over breakfast.

aiming them into a box. She soon tired of this and climbed to the top of an apple tree, where she found a dozen apples that hadn't fallen and began throwing them at Joe. When she came down she made him race her three times round the garden. Before he started his third round, Minna had finished and was doing a handstand on the wall.

"Look!" she commanded from her upside-down position. "The wall's so wide I think I can walk on my hands."

"Oh," Joe said, dismayed by the prospect of her falling into the monster's garden.

But at that moment two men came out of the monster's back door. They wore helmets and orange jackets, and they walked between the neat rows of cabbages and broccoli, muttering in deep, unfriendly voices.

Minna jumped down from the wall and Joe moved closer to her. As the men approached the owl-tree he caught his breath. The tree was whispering urgently but Joe couldn't understand its message. He only knew the tree felt threatened, for every golden leaf was trembling.

The men stood under the branches and looked up into the restless leaves. One brought out a metal tape and wrapped it round the great, grey trunk. He did this carelessly, as though the tree had no feeling.

"What are they doing?" Joe asked Minna, his voice very faint. He knew the men were enemies.

Minna shrugged. "Let's ask Gran," she said.

Something had happened to Granny Diamond. They found her sitting at the kitchen table staring at her clasped hands with glittery blue eyes.

"What is it, Gran?" Joe asked. "What's happening?"

Granny Diamond took a moment to find words, and then she said, "He's going to cut down the owl-tree!"

"The monster?"

"Monster, yes," said Granny Diamond. "That's what he is, a monster. He's mentioned the tree before, but I didn't think he was serious. Now the date is fixed. They're coming on Friday, with their saws and ladders and goodness knows what else... He couldn't look me in the eye, so he rang me up. 'It'll fall in the field,' he says, 'but keep the children out of the garden, just in case.' I begged him not to. 'It's not dangerous,' I said. 'It's not a problem, it's a good tree, a beautiful tree, the garden will be empty without it … the world won't be the same.' "

"And what did he say?" Minna sat beside her.

"Took no notice. Acted as if I hadn't spoken. 'It casts a shadow,' he says, 'over my vegetable plot. I can't grow onions or salad or peas and the flowers all lean away from it. The tree is stifling them.' "

"He's got a point," said Minna. "There aren't many flowers in his back garden."

"Minna, how dare you!" Granny Diamond cried. "His front garden is full of colour."

There was a knock on the front door and Minna flew off, partly to escape Granny Diamond's glare.

Joe heard boys' voices in the hall and Minna saying, "Joe wouldn't like it. He's scared of heights." She brought the Ludd twins into the kitchen and asked if she could go round to their house.

"Well…" Granny Diamond was uncertain.

"Please," begged Minna.

"It's only at the end of the lane," said Ian. "And

we'll bring her back in an hour."

"You're staying in the house then, not going off somewhere else?" Granny Diamond asked the twins.

"We've got a tree-house," Roger said proudly. "We don't want to go anywhere else."

So Granny Diamond gave her permission and Minna and the boys ran off all talking at once. The twins hadn't even looked in Joe's direction. For them, it seemed, he didn't exist.

"I expect they thought you were too young to join in." Granny Diamond smiled at Joe.

"They didn't want me," Joe said. "And even if they did, I wouldn't have gone." This wasn't strictly true. It was only the tree-house that had worried him. "I'm scared of falling, Gran," he confessed. "Why is that?"

"Everyone's afraid of something," she told him.

"Not Minna."

"I think you'll find she is."

Granny Diamond got up and went to the window. She gazed out at the owl-tree, her pale eyes wandering along every branch, as though she were being surprised all over again, by its shape and its strength.

"How can he kill it?" she murmured, and Joe thought he heard a tiny crack, somewhere deep inside her, like a diamond breaking.

"What shall I do without it?" she said. "The fields won't look the same, nor will my garden. And the clouds will all rush in at me."

Joe pictured an army of thunderclouds sweeping across the landscape with nothing to stop them. He closed his eyes and saw the tree falling, heard its dying groan. But when he blinked them open the tree was still there and very much alive.

"There's still a chance, Gran," he said. "Perhaps we can save the tree."

Granny Diamond's shoulders sagged. "His mind's made up." Already she seemed to have withered a little. Without the owl-tree she might fade away altogether. "How can we save it, Joe?" she said.

Joe didn't know how, just yet. He would have to visit the monster. He would have to look him in the eye, which might be like a dragon's eye, fiery and paralysing. And he would have to make the monster change his mind. But Joe wasn't good at explaining things. He would have to get Minna to help him.

The day had been bright with sunshine but now raindrops speckled the window-pane and a spiteful wind was plucking at the owl-tree's leaves.

"I'll save you," Joe murmured. "I promise."

CHAPTER FOUR

True to their word, the twins brought Minna back an hour later. They came bouncing into the kitchen, where Joe had been chopping onions for Granny Diamond. He saw the others through a mist of tears and desperately wiped his face. The twins rushed off with a quick, "See you, Minna," before Joe had time to explain his red eyes.

"It's the onions," Joe told Minna, in case she thought he'd been crying. "What did you do at the Ludds' place?"

"We sat in the tree-house and played a game. We were goblins and wizards, that sort of thing."

"Was it high, the tree-house?"

"Very, very high. I had to climb a knotted rope to get there. You wouldn't have liked it, Joe."

Joe saw the others through a mist of tears
and desperately wiped his face.

"I might've," he said. But the thought of clinging to a rope while the ground swung far below made him feel dizzy.

Over by the stove, Granny Diamond slowly stirred a pan of something. When Minna spoke to her she didn't seem to hear, so Minna tapped her on the shoulder and she jumped round with a gasp, dropping the spoon on the floor.

"Are you all right, Gran?" asked Minna, picking up the spoon. "You look all … peculiar."

"Of course I'm all right," she snapped, and she plonked her saucepan on the draining-board and left the room.

"What's up with Gran?" asked Minna. "She never gets bad-tempered."

"It's the tree," Joe told her. "The tree and the monster."

"Why should an old tree make her act peculiar?"

Joe was astonished. "The monster's going to chop it down. Didn't you hear what Gran said?"

"It's not as if it's in her garden," Minna said carelessly. "What difference will it make to Gran?"

"It's everything to her," Joe said. "The tree's in her window. She sees it all day. She watches it when she's alone … it talks to her."

"You're not making sense, Joe." Minna pranced round the room, picking up a biscuit, tapping her fingers on cupboards, rattling a drawer. Joe felt like sticking a pin in her, or nailing her foot to the floor. He was surprised how angry he felt and how desperate. He had to get Minna to take the situation seriously.

"I'm going to visit the monster," he said, "maybe this afternoon, will you come?"

"I'm busy," she said in an offhand way.

"You're scared."

"Of course I'm not scared."

"You are!"

"Joe, you know very well I'm not scared." Minna stopped moving at last. "I just don't want to visit a silly old man who's going to chop down a tree."

"You're scared of his face and what he might do to you!"

"Come off it, Joe!" His sister whirled away. "It's you

who's scared." The scornful words came winging through the open door as Minna ran upstairs.

Joe crumpled into a chair. All his brave intentions were melting away. But when he saw Granny Diamond scattering breadcrumbs under the owl-tree, and looking skyward with a face as pale as ivory, he knew he must do something.

He chose late afternoon. It would be almost dark, yet clear enough for him to see his way up to the monster's door.

And if he stayed outside in the dusky garden, maybe the monster wouldn't see him properly, and the ugly face wouldn't seem so frightening.

Granny Diamond had fallen asleep by the fire when Joe slipped out of the house. Minna was upstairs listening to music. Joe closed the front door quietly and walked down to the gate. Clouds of leaves spiralled from the rowan tree and the brown, velvety ground deadened his footsteps. He reached the monster's gate and took a deep breath of autumn air, hoping it was full of courage. And then he was on the neat stone path that led to the monster's door.

Joe found himself facing a brass knocker in the shape of a lion's head. He couldn't touch it. He stepped back and scanned the windows. The house was in darkness, its owner asleep, perhaps. How could Joe rouse a sleeping monster? The rage would be terrible.

But he wouldn't give up, not yet. He crept round to the side of the house where a strip of light shone from a window. Joe moved closer to the source of light and peered through a gap between two heavy curtains. Soon his face was almost touching the glass pane, and the details of the room beyond swam into focus.

He saw a log fire, walls covered in pictures and, on a small table, a photograph of a boy in a silver frame. In every picture there was an aeroplane. There were small silvery planes, rising, diving and fighting; there were bombers and young pilots in leather jackets and tight-fitting helmets. One of the pictures showed a plane falling out of the sky, with its tail blazing. It was a coloured picture and the flames were painted in brilliant colours.

Joe was so intrigued by the pictures that he didn't

*Joe crept round to the side of the house and peered
through a gap between two heavy curtains.*

notice the man in the room until he leaned out of his chair to poke the fire. Joe blinked, dreading to see the monster's face, but the man had his back to the window and all Joe could see was a head of tousled grey hair, rather in need of a cut. It curled right over the collar of his shabby tweed jacket.

In his head, Joe practised the words he wanted to say. He began to feel confident. Perhaps it wouldn't be difficult after all. But then the monster heaved himself out of the chair, growing taller and taller and taller. His shadow climbed across the wall, plunging the shiny glass-covered pictures into gloom. And then the monster turned towards the window, and Joe fell back with a cry.

Bent almost double, Joe shuffled away, hoping he wouldn't be seen. When he reached the corner of the house he ran, heart pounding, across the murky lawn and hurled himself at the gate.

As he tumbled into the lane a deep voice barked, "Who's there?"

Chapter Five

Joe rolled in dead leaves, his eyes shut tight, pretending he didn't exist, so that nothing could hurt him.

But he hadn't been followed. No heavy footsteps trod the monster's path. The lane was silent except for a slight rustling near Joe's head. He froze as a breath of warm air drifted over his forehead. He brought up his hands to cover his face and encountered a wet sort of roughness. Joe gave a scream of terror.

"Get off, Ludwig," said the voice of someone very young.

Joe opened his eyes. He saw a black shaggy dog and a boy. The boy was quite small and Joe thought he recognized him.

Joe rolled in dead leaves, his eyes shut tight,
pretending he didn't exist.

"Ludwig's just nosy," said the boy. "He wouldn't hurt anyone."

Joe got to his feet, feeling rather foolish. Now he could see the small boy a little better. "Are you Alex?" he asked.

The boy nodded.

"And your dog's called Ludwig."

"Yes, because we're Ludds. It's a good name, isn't it? You're supposed to pronounce it Loodvig, but we don't."

Joe suddenly felt responsible. "It's nearly dark. Does your mum know where you are?"

Alex avoided the question. "Ludwig needed exercise," he said, "and no one else would take him out."

"Shall I walk back with you?"

"Why were you curled up in the leaves?" asked Alex, who, it seemed, didn't like answering questions. "Were you hiding?"

"Sort of," Joe admitted.

"From the monster?" Alex began to shuffle away and Joe ran to catch up with him.

"It was a game, really." Joe fell into step beside the boy and Alex let Ludwig race ahead, dragging his lead through the leaves.

"It was a deadly game, wasn't it?" Alex said gravely.

"Yes," said Joe. "A matter of life and death," and he found himself telling Alex about Granny Diamond and the tree that meant so much to her. "I don't know how to stop the monster killing the owl-tree," he said, "and my gran says she can't live without it."

"Is she old?"

"Very old. She's really our great-grandmother. I think the owl-tree talks to her, but my sister doesn't believe me."

"I believe you," Alex said.

They had reached the Ludds' gate and Ludwig was whining for it to be opened. When Alex lifted the latch, the dog nosed through and rushed up to the house. But Alex stood a moment, staring at Joe. It was now so dark Joe could hardly see his face.

"Has the tree ever talked to you?" Alex spoke in a hushed voice.

"Not yet," Joe said.

"I wonder if it will," Alex murmured, and he ran to his front door. He had to stand on tiptoe to reach the bell. A woman opened the door and pulled him inside, saying something in a high, worried voice.

As Joe walked back to Granny Diamond's he found himself in the path of a huge corn-coloured moon, and he began to run, hoping it would stay just where it was so he could show his gran and cheer her up a bit.

When he got in, Minna was on the telephone, telling their dad about the Ludds' tree-house. As Joe ran past he heard his dad say, "My little tomboy!" Tomboy was his pet name for Minna. Joe sometimes wondered about that. After all, he was the boy, but no one gave him a special name. He was just Joe.

Granny Diamond did not seem interested in Joe's moon. "Don't you want to speak to Dad?" she asked.

"Minna's going to be ages," Joe told her. "Please come and see the moon while I wait for my turn."

Granny Diamond smiled at last. "All right, Joe," she said.

He ran ahead, past Minna, hopping from one foot

to the other but still talking, and opened the front door. The corn-gold moon was rising but to see it at its best they would have to go into the lane. When Joe reached the gate he turned and saw Granny Diamond on the step, leaning on a stick. He had never seen her with a stick before, and it gave him a cold, scary feeling. Joe ran back. "The moon's getting higher," he said. "Soon you'll be able to see it from the door!"

Minna yelled that Dad wanted him on the phone, but when he took the receiver he kept his eye on his gran. She seemed a bit fuzzy round the edges, not as bright and straight-backed as she used to be.

His father's voice said, "You there, Joe!"

"Hello, Dad!"

"Everything all right? You sound very faint."

How could Joe explain to someone far away that Granny Diamond didn't look too well? How could he tell Dad about a tree that meant so much to Gran; without it she might fade away? He had a go, even though the task seemed hopeless.

"I'm all right, but there's this tree that Gran's

neighbour wants to chop down. He's a monster, Dad!"

"The tree?"

"No, the man next door. I don't know how to … how to…"

"Ask Minna, Joe. She'll know what to do."

Joe couldn't tell his dad that Minna wasn't interested.

"The baby will be born any day now," his dad went on. "Mum sends her love and says you must think of some names."

"Me?" Joe was surprised.

"You, Joe. Minna chose your name. Now it's your turn."

Joe didn't know how to take this news. He ought to say something to let Dad know he was pleased, but Granny Diamond was making signs at him so he just said, "Bye, Dad, Gran wants to talk to you!" and he went to find his sister.

Minna was sitting on her bed wearing headphones. At first she wouldn't take any notice of Joe, but when she saw that he wasn't going to leave until she talked to him she snatched off the headphones and said, "What?"

"I'm supposed to think of names," Joe said, "for the baby. I can think of boys' names, but I'm no good on girls'."

"It's not my problem," said Minna airily. "They can call it Bonzo for all I care."

"Bonzo? That's a dog's name."

"I don't *mean* Bonzo, silly. You think of something. Ask Gran."

Granny Diamond was in the kitchen. Outside, the garden lay in a heavy, secret sort of darkness. Nothing could be seen, for the moon wasn't yet high enough. But Joe knew his gran's eyes were fixed on the owl-tree. "What am I going to do?" she murmured.

Joe felt ashamed. If only he'd tapped on the monster's window and said the things he'd planned. He knew he would never do that now. "If I was brave I could save the tree," he said, "but I'm too scared, Gran. I'll never be brave."

Granny Diamond gave him a sudden hug. "People

who are scared are sometimes the bravest of all," she said. "We've got four days left to find a solution."

Four days. There was still time. When Joe was getting ready for bed he tried to think of possible ways to save the tree. But there seemed to be no answer. Perhaps it was time for the owl-tree to talk to him. Joe opened the window. With half-closed eyes he peered into the night and asked, "What shall I do? Tell me?"

A mysterious sound stirred the air; a soft yet urgent whisper. "Joe...oh...oh...oh!" It rose and fell, now distant, now close to his ear, an ancient voice, secret and wise.

"I can hear you," Joe called. "Tell me how to save you!"

Out of the darkness came a different voice. A scream that made Joe reel back, shaking with fright. But worse than the scream was the ghostly shape that flashed by his window.

CHAPTER SIX

"Gran!" Joe cried. "Minna! Gran!"

They both came at once, colliding in the doorway, Gran out of breath and Minna frowning.

"There's a ghost outside!" Joe told them. "Pale and horrible."

Minna looked out. "Well, it's gone now," she said.

"Perhaps it was moonlight," Granny Diamond suggested. "Or leaves floating past." She closed the window and drew the curtains.

"Whatever it was, it's outside now and you're in, Joe. So nothing can hurt you."

"It screamed," Joe whispered.

"You've got the wrong day, Joe. It's not Hallowe'en any more." Minna sidled out with an unkind snigger.

Granny Diamond tucked Joe into bed and turned out the light. She left his door open so she could hear if he called her again. But she was walking so slowly Joe didn't think she would reach him in time to help.

In the room across the passage, Minna took a crumpled sheet of paper from under her pillow. She had written twelve names on the paper, girls' names in a neat column. She'd put them down for Joe but to Minna they were like the words of a bad spell. She wanted Mum to have another boy. If she didn't, Minna would have to be a tomboy for ever. And she was getting fed up with it. She wanted to be someone different, someone clever or musical like her friend Lucille. Secretly Minna longed to be an angel in the Christmas play, an angel like the one that hung over her bed. But who else would take on the job of family tomboy? Not Joe, who couldn't even climb a tree.

She pushed the list of names under her pillow and went to draw her curtains. But as she reached the window, something pale loomed out of the darkness. Minna saw the beat of angel's wings, heard a wild and chilling cry, and almost screamed herself. But flinging her hand across her mouth, she tumbled back on to the bed.

So there *was* a ghost out there! Joe's ghost.

Next morning they had an almost silent breakfast. Minna seemed to be weighed down with secret thoughts and Granny Diamond was stooped and sleepy. The fog outside was so thick they couldn't even see the wall, and the owl-tree had completely vanished.

Had the monster felled the tree in the night? Was that why it had cried out? Joe didn't dare ask Granny Diamond, she wasn't herself at all.

As soon as breakfast was over he stole out of the back door and into the white mist beyond. Stepping carefully on to the path he began to make his way to the end of the garden. When he still couldn't see the tree or the wall, he stumbled forward, afraid of falling but desperate to see what lay behind the mist. He was almost there when a great branch loomed into view.

Joe heaved himself on to the wall and found that the branch came just above his waist. It would have been easy to swing himself over it, and to sit there bravely.

But he wasn't quite ready for that. He just held tight to the branch and gazed at the top of the owl-tree. The fog had enclosed it in a cold blanket, but here inside, where the trunk wound up to the sky, it was warm and bright, and Joe could see hundreds of birds, some flickering between the leaves and others tapping at the trunk. A few sat very still regarding Joe with bright inquisitive eyes. What did they know?

From the top of the tree came a strange rustling murmur, "Here ... here ... here..." The owl-tree had a secret, right at the top, and Joe would have to get it. But not yet.

When he got back to the house the kitchen seemed full of people. The Ludd twins were there with their mother. Minna was throwing things into a bag.

Mrs Ludd was surprised to see Joe. "Oh," she said. "They didn't tell me about you. Are you Minna's brother? Or..."

Minna said, "He's called Joe."

"Minna's going to spend the day with us," Mrs Ludd told Joe. "Do you want to come?"

Minna and the twins weren't interested in his

answer. They were chatting together in a corner. Joe shook his head.

Mrs Ludd smiled invitingly. "Are you sure?"

"No, thanks," Joe said. He had to think about the owl-tree, lay his plans.

Granny Diamond didn't see her visitors out. She stayed where she was, huddled in an easy chair. "My bones are playing up today," she said. "What are you going to do?"

"Plenty," Joe said.

The fog began to lift. Joe spent most of the day staring up into the owl-tree, counting the branches and trying to guess the distances between them.

Minna came back after tea. She couldn't stop talking about her wonderful day. When it grew dark Joe began to have second thoughts about his plan. But he heard Granny Diamond heave a sigh as she shuffled close to the stove, and he knew he would have to go through with it. She was fading before their eyes.

Minna's busy day had made her so tired she went to bed much earlier than usual. Joe followed, leaving

Granny Diamond to read a paper by the fire. He didn't undress when he got to his room. He sat on his bed, waiting to put his plan into action. He chose the night for its darkness and secrecy. The monster wouldn't see him.

When the house was quiet, Joe crept downstairs. It was a cold, clear night and the sky was glittering with stars. But Joe didn't stop to look at them. He walked purposefully down to the owl-tree. This time, when he had pulled himself on to the wall, he swung one leg over the branch that leaned, so helpfully, within reach. Now that he was actually on the tree, with the rough bark under his hands and his feet swinging free, he found that he didn't dread the adventure ahead. The touch of the tree made everything possible.

Joe drew his feet on to the branch and crawled closer to the trunk.

The owl-tree shone pearl-grey in the night, its golden leaves turned to silver. Joe found a foot-hold and began to climb. The tree slipped branches under his feet and swept them close to his hands. Joe pulled himself up to the sky. Higher and higher. Now the houses were far

Joe pulled himself up to the sky. Higher and higher.
Now the houses were far below.

below and he could see chinks of light from bedroom windows.

"I'm here," Joe told the tree. "So tell me how to save you." The tree whispered and sighed, "Higher... Higher..." How high would he have to go before he had an answer? He put his ear against the trunk and heard a heartbeat deep inside.

"Tell me," Joe begged.

There was a movement above him, the beginning of an answer. And then it came – a shriek and a wild, white thrashing over his head. And Joe, too frightened to cry out, was falling, falling, falling!

CHAPTER SEVEN

As Joe fell earthwards, small branches slid into his hands. The tree was trying to save him. His fall wasn't as bad as it might have been, but his frightened fingers lost their grip on the lowest branch, and he crashed on to the ground.

For a moment he lay quite still. His knee and his shoulder ached, so he slowly rolled on to his back. And then he saw that he was on the wrong side of the wall. He had fallen into the monster's garden!

He felt too bruised and dizzy to climb the wall again, and wondered if he could creep back past the monster's house. He got to his feet, legs a bit shaky, and found his shadow lying beside another, a long shadow that moved beside him like a widening chasm.

Joe turned to face the monster.

He tried to give an explanation but no words came.

The monster said, "Tom?"

Joe shook his head. Still no words came. He was glad the tall man's face was in shadow. The monster took a step towards him and Joe, rooted to the ground, looked away and up at the stars that spun round and round and round. And then he fell a second time.

When he opened his eyes he was being carried through Granny Diamond's gate. A gruff voice above him called, "Mrs Diamond. I've got your boy!"

A startled Granny Diamond opened the front door. "Bring him in here," she said. "Oh, Joe, Joe, whatever have you… Oh dear, oh dear."

Joe was lowered on to the sofa and, finding a voice at last, said, "I'm sorry." He looked straight at Granny Diamond and tried to keep the monster out of his sight.

Minna appeared in the doorway, yawning. "What's happened?" she asked.

"Joe fell out of the tree," the gruff voice said.

Joe allowed himself a quick glimpse of the monster, and was astonished to see a face like any other. Old, yes, and wrinkled, but rather fine for all that. Joe could only see one side, however; perhaps the other...

"Joe doesn't climb trees," Minna said. "He can't," she added.

"Of course, he can!" There was a touch of thunder in the monster's tone. He turned to Minna, and Joe was too late to look away. He saw the monster as he really was. Not ugly, or even scary. The two sides of his face didn't match, that was all. One side was pale, the other coloured by a dark shadow.

"Why did you do it, Joe?" Granny Diamond was asking. "Why?"

Joe said, "I thought the owl-tree could tell me how to save it. It must know more than we do, being so old. There's a secret up there somewhere."

"Oh, Joe," she gave a weary sigh.

And then he remembered that the tree *had* answered him. "I saw it!" he said joyfully. "That's the tree's secret – an owl. A great, great owl, with pale wings and a face ... like a flower." He heard the monster's intake of breath and saw a fist clenched tighter. "Gran, it's just like you said. It *is* an owl-tree!"

"Why did you do it, Joe?" Granny Diamond
was asking. "Why?"

"Oh," said Minna, then shut her mouth tight.

"A barn owl," cried Granny Diamond happily. "Great, pale wings, you said."

"There are no barn owls here," growled the monster. "They went years ago, when all the farm buildings came down. No barns, no owls."

"Excuse me," said Granny Diamond huffily. "They've built special owl-houses on poles in one of the fields near the village. Two families nested there last spring. The barn owls are coming back."

"Rubbish!" snapped the monster.

Joe swung his feet to the floor. "It's true," he said looking the monster in the eye. "That's why I fell. The owl screamed at me. Its wings were so pale," he flung out his arms, "and so big. It flew past my window last night and I thought it was a ghost."

"Of course, the screech," said Granny Diamond. "Now, there's proof, Mr Rock. Barn owls screech, they don't hoot!"

"Yes! Yes!" Joe watched the monster, whose eyes weren't fiery, but more the colour of a sad grey sea. "So you can't kill the tree because the owl lives there!"

"So this is what it's all about." The monster's face took on a stormy look. "The tree's coming down, that's final."

"But the owl…" said Joe.

"Look, boy. If there is an owl you'd better keep away. Owls are wild, fierce creatures. Eyes have been lost, cheeks torn. Owls are predators, not fluffy toys."

"I'm not afraid," Joe muttered.

"You should be."

"Couldn't you … re-consider?" begged Granny Diamond.

"I'll bid you goodnight." The monster brushed past Minna, who scurried into the room.

"Mr Rock," called Granny Diamond. "I didn't thank you…" She tottered into the hall, but the monster had gone.

As the front door closed, a draught sped into the sitting-room, fanning the flames in the grate, and in the firelight Joe thought he could see a burning plane and a man tumbling out of it.

Minna said, "Did you really climb the tree?"

"Yes."

She gave him a puzzled sort of frown. "You are strange, Joe. Fancy climbing a tree at night." When she left the room she didn't look scornful anymore.

As Minna mounted the stairs, she thought about the great wings outside her window. Perhaps, after all, it wasn't impossible for her to be an angel in the Christmas play.

Granny Diamond brought Joe a mug of cocoa. "You must never, never do that again, Joe," she said. "Whatever possessed you?"

"Someone had to do it," he told her. "And I thought I'd found the answer, Gran. Because the owl was a sign, wasn't it, that the tree mustn't be chopped down."

"I'm afraid my neighbour doesn't see it that way," said Granny Diamond. "Nothing can save the tree now."

Joe should have felt defeated. But he didn't. He knew he'd come close to a secret, but not close enough. It was hidden in the monster's strange sad face, and Joe meant to find it.

CHAPTER EIGHT

A day passed.

Minna spent a great deal of time with the Ludds. She told everyone she met that Joe had climbed the tree. "Right to the top," she boasted, though she didn't know this for a fact.

Alex brought Ludwig round to see Joe, and Granny Diamond let them eat cookies beneath the owl-tree.

"Is the monster still going to chop it down?" Alex asked.

Joe said, "I've got two days left to make him change his mind. Tomorrow I'm going to see him. Today, I'm just gathering my strength."

"Aren't you scared?"

"A bit. But I'm still going."

Granny Diamond let them eat cookies
beneath the owl-tree.

In the afternoon they raked up the leaves that covered Granny Diamond's garden. They made big rustling heaps that Ludwig kept bouncing into, scattering them in all directions. Joe and Alex rolled in the leaves, breathless with laughter.

That night Joe heard the owl's ghostly screech, but the sky looked dark and empty. It's out there, somewhere, Joe thought, and it can save the tree. But I'm not sure how. In his mind he climbed the tree again, seeing the shape of branches and shadows, feeling the rough wood. And he saw the great wings and the fierce, flower-like face; and this time he remembered the deadly talons, and an odd detail that he'd half forgotten – a greyish green ring just above the owl's foot.

Joe fell asleep wondering what the ring could mean.

"They ring birds to keep track of them," Granny Diamond told him at breakfast. "To find out where they're breeding and how long they live. That sort of thing."

"How long do barn owls live?" asked Joe.

"Twenty years maybe. But that doesn't happen very often. There isn't enough food for them. They like big fields of long wild grass for hunting in, and tons of mice and voles to eat."

"Yuk," said Minna. "Are you coming to see the bonfire, Joe? They finished it yesterday. It's ginormous."

"I'm busy," he told her.

"You're very mysterious these days," Minna remarked.

After breakfast Joe caught Granny Diamond on her own. "I'm going to see the monster," he said. "There's something I forgot to tell him."

"It's no use," she said. "He'll never change his mind." And she gave one of her rattly coughs.

"I've got to try!" Joe winked and gave the thumbs up sign, which brought a smile to Granny Diamond's face and gave him confidence.

This time he walked boldly up the monster's path. When he rapped the lion's head knocker, he braced himself for the monster's roar.

But the man who opened the door looked solemn

and tired. "Oh, it's you," he muttered. "And what do you want?"

Joe swallowed hard. "A chat."

The monster frowned. "Hmph!" and pulled the door wider. Joe stepped into a dark hall, rather like Granny Diamond's.

"In here, Joe." When the monster spoke his name it sounded friendly.

They sat in the room full of pictures, in big armchairs on either side of the fire.

"Well?" the monster said.

"It's about the tree." Joe waited for an interruption but the monster just turned his head so that only the good side of his face could be seen. Joe looked round the room, searching for a way to begin, and saw the picture of a plane on fire. "My gran says you're a very brave man, a hero, so you probably weren't afraid of falling. But I'm not brave. I know what it's like to be frightened of falling. How d'you know the tree's not afraid? It's a long way for a tall tree to fall."

The monster didn't move a muscle.

"If the tree dies maybe the owl will too!" Joe went

on. "And if there's no owl there'll be no owlets."

"If there *is* an owl, it could roost in another tree," the monster pointed out.

"Why not your tree? My gran is frightened of being without it."

"Huh!" This wasn't a laugh. The man couldn't even smile. Perhaps it hurt his face too much.

Joe couldn't think of a better way to put things. He began to feel angry with himself and with the monster. And then he remembered the ring. "It's a special owl," he said. "It's got a ring round its leg."

Now he had the full glare of the monster's mismatching face, but instead of frightening Joe it made him feel bold. "I did see a barn owl. I did! I did!" He kicked the chair with his heel. "And it had a ring on. It did! It did!"

The monster stood up. He towered above Joe, and Joe shrank back afraid he'd gone too far. But the man started walking round the room and talking in a voice that was slow and sort of far away.

"There was an owl," he said. "An owlet. We found it by the old barn after a storm. The parents had abandoned the nest so we brought it back, fed it with a dropper and kept it warm. It was an ugly little thing, just a mass of untidy feathers. Tom was determined it should survive and it did. It grew into a beautiful bird. When it could fly we ringed it so that we should know if the same owl came back. And, for a while, it did. It used to roost in the big tree." He seemed to have run out of words and just stood looking through the window, at the tree where his owl used to sit.

"Who's Tom?" Joe ventured.

"My grandson."

"His owl's come back, then."

"It's impossible."

"No." Joe jumped out of the chair. "It's Tom's owl. You ought to tell him."

"Look, Joe, all this was fifteen years ago. My grandson is a grown man. He's in America. And the owl you think you saw isn't the same as ours. It can't be. It's been dead a long time."

"Maybe not. If it's not the same owl, then perhaps it's a ghost. It's trying to tell you something and you ought to listen." Joe made for the door.

There was nothing else he could do.

He heard the monster's tread behind him, but he didn't look back until he was on the step outside, and then he saw how weary the monster looked. "There's something you ought to know, Joe. I was afraid of falling. In fact I was never more frightened of anything in my life."

"You?" Joe was astonished. "But you're a hero."

The monster shrugged and suddenly Joe found himself asking, "Are you coming to the bonfire tomorrow? My sister says it's ginormous."

"I don't go out much. People think I'm a bit of a monster." Mr Rock began to close the door.

"Well, you're not," said Joe. He ran down the path wondering if he'd said too much, or not enough, to save the owl-tree.

CHAPTER NINE

Minna was swinging on Granny Diamond's gate. "Dad's been on the phone," she said. "The baby's come, and it's a girl."

"Oh," Joe wondered how this new baby would change things. "I don't know any girls' names."

"Here!" Minna shoved a crumpled piece of paper at him. "I've put down twelve names. You've only got to choose one."

"Thanks!" He took the paper and they walked up to the house together. The wind blew leaves in their faces and snatched at their hair, and Joe said, "You didn't want a sister, did you?"

"I've changed my mind."

Before they went in, Minna suddenly tugged at

Joe's shoulder and asked, rather shyly for her, "Would I look funny dressed as an angel?"

"No."

"With wings an' all. D'you think I could be an angel in the Christmas play?"

" 'Course you could," he told her.

Granny Diamond chattered happily about the new baby, her plum-coloured eyes, and fluffy blonde hair, but when she looked at Joe her face was full of questions.

"I don't know if I said the right things to Mr Rock," he told her.

"We'll just have to wait then, won't we," she said.

The wind intensified; Granny Diamond's house echoed with creaks and rattles. A storm of leaves blew about fields and gardens and the sky was crowded with fluttering, agitated birds. The owl-tree moaned like a troubled ocean as its red and gold leaves were torn away. But when the pattern of bare branches emerged, Joe thought the tree looked rather grand and dignified. Now he could see a deep hollow in the side, where, perhaps, the barn owl roosted.

"The wind's blowing right through me," Granny Diamond complained. "I swear I'm full of holes."

She sat by the fire with a rug tucked round her knees while Joe and Minna watched a television film about elephants.

At night Joe heard the barn owl's screech above the wind. There was no mistaking it. He wondered if Mr Rock could hear the owl, or had he covered his ears so the sound wouldn't reach him? Joe opened his window and put out his head. Craning into the wind he could see the wall of Mr Rock's house. There was a soft glow coming from a downstairs room.

At the end of the garden the owl-tree thrashed and moaned as though it were at war. A pale shape soared out of it, swung through the stormy night and dropped into the beam of light from Mr Rock's window. It hung there, like a frozen angel, its white wings gleaming, and then it vanished.

Joe closed his window and got into bed. Had Mr Rock seen the owl and understood its message? For a

A pale shape soared out of the owl-tree
and through the stormy night.

long time Joe lay awake, listening to the mysterious taps and creaks as sleepless Granny Diamond wandered through her house.

Next morning she didn't come down for breakfast. Joe and Minna found her sitting up in bed with a shawl round her shoulders. "Silly me," she said. "I went to bed too late, and now my bones are aching."

The children got their own breakfast and took Granny Diamond a tray of tea and toast. But she wasn't hungry. Her face was chalky white and her thin hands moved restlessly over the covers. She rang Mrs Ludd from the telephone by her bed and asked if Minna and Joe could come over for the day.

"I can't go," Joe told her. "They're coming for the tree and I want to be here."

"Joe," she said sternly. "You must go. I need a rest."

Mrs Ludd came for them after breakfast, and really it wasn't too bad. The wind had blown itself out and it was a day of sunshine, showers and rainbows. Roger and Ian invited Joe up to their tree-house, but he played football with Alex and Ludwig instead. Ludwig couldn't be hauled up the tree, Alex said, and he was cross if they left him alone on the ground.

There was a large box of fireworks sitting beside the Ludds' front door, ready for the bonfire party. "But I'm not coming," Alex told Joe. "Someone's got to stay with Ludwig, he hates fireworks."

"Can't he stay by himself?" Joe asked.

"No." And then Alex admitted that he was frightened of fireworks too. "The bangs make me jump," he said, "and the twins always laugh at me."

"But I'll be there and I won't laugh," Joe said.

Alex looked suspicious and didn't answer.

Thunder rumbled in the clouds and Joe wondered if he'd hear the crack of the owl-tree when it fell. He kept listening for it and by the afternoon he couldn't bear waiting any longer. He decided to tell Mrs Ludd the truth, that Granny Diamond was ill because the owl-tree was coming down, and he wanted to be there when it happened.

"But Joe that's terrible, " said Mrs Ludd.

"We'll come with you," said Roger. "We'll climb the tree like motorway protestors!"

"Don't you dare," said Mrs Ludd. "You've been warned to keep away." But she let them walk up the lane, just to see what was happening. There was a yellow van parked outside the monster's gate, with a huge mechanical digger behind it.

"Wow!" Ian exclaimed. "A digger!"

"What's that for?" asked Minna.

"It's a big tree," Ian said, "so tree-surgeons have to saw off some of the branches before it falls. Then they chop it up in sections and dig up the roots. They must have taken the digger into the field."

Joe felt sick. Until now he hadn't really believed it would happen.

There was no one in the van or in the cabin of the digger, and Roger wanted to climb up and drive the digger away, but Minna held him back. "Look out," she said. "They're coming back."

Three men in orange boilersuits came down the monster's path. They didn't look happy. The children scurried into Granny Diamond's garden and stood behind the gate.

Two of the men jumped into the van and drove off,

the third climbed into the digger and took a moment to start the engine. At last the big machine spluttered into life and rumbled past the children. It was so wide it almost filled the lane.

"Let's go and see what they've done," said Minna.

They trooped around Granny Diamond's house and into the back garden. Joe came last, afraid of what he might see. Just before he turned the corner he closed his eyes.

"Look!" yelled Minna, and Joe's eyes flew open.

The owl-tree towered into a fiery sky, its dark limbs sharp against the sunset. And everybody cheered. Joe forgot that Granny Diamond wasn't well. He rushed to the back door and flung it open. "Gran!" he shouted. And there she was, standing by the cooker, her face all rosy from the oven.

"I feel so much better," she said.

"The tree – it's still there," cried Joe, "and the men have gone away."

The other children crowded in behind him. "Are they coming back? Why didn't they chop it down?"

Granny Diamond's eyes were sparkling. "Mr Rock

has changed his mind," she told them. "He called to tell me about an hour ago. I don't know what you said to him, Joe, but whatever it was, you saved the owl-tree."

Roger yelled, "Joe, the hero!"

Joe shook his head. "The owl saved the tree," he said.

Chapter Ten

It was a grand bonfire party, but Ludwig was wise to stay at home. The boom of fireworks was enough to make a dog jump out of its skin. The sky blazed with exploding stars, rockets with fiery tails roared over the fields and shrieking sparks whirled round in brilliant colours.

Joe and Alex watched from the back of the crowd and, although Alex gasped a couple of times, he stood his ground and didn't once cover his ears.

Towards the end of the firework display something made Joe glance down the lane. Two shadowy figures stood by the hedge. One tall and one small. Granny Diamond and Mr Rock? They turned and walked away before he could be sure. But when Joe asked her

*Joe glanced down the lane. Two shadowy figures
stood by the hedge. One tall and one small.*

later if she'd seen the bonfire she said, "To tell the truth we did just take a peep. I wouldn't have missed it for anything."

Before they went to bed, Granny Diamond called Joe and Minna into her room. "Look!" she said. "Quickly, before it's gone!"

They ran and pushed their faces against her window, and saw the barn owl's ivory wings gliding over the moonlit field.

"It's hunting," whispered Granny Diamond.

The owl dropped, suddenly, into the long grass, then rose and swung away. Now it swooped towards them, flew high into the old tree and, perching on a branch, began to eat its prey. It was then that Joe saw Mr Rock in his garden, gazing at the owl-tree.

And this time the owl-tree wasn't afraid.